NIKI DALY has won many awards for his exuberant work. His groundbreaking *Not So fast Songololo* (1986), winner of a US Parent's Choice Award, paved the way for post-apartheid South African children's books. Since then, he has been published across the globe and has visited and presented talks in several countries. *Once Upon a Time* was an Honor Winner in the US Children's Africana Book Awards of 2004. *Jamela's Dress* – first in the Jamela series – was another milestone book, chosen by the ALA as a Notable Children's Book and by Booklist as one of the Top 10 African American Picture Books of 2000, and winning both the Children's Literature Choice Award and the Parent's Choice Silver Award. Niki lives with his wife, the illustrator Jude Daly, in Mowbray, a bustling Cape Town suburb.

Once Upon

For my dear friend Ann – with love from Niki

First published in Great Britain in 2003 by
Frances Lincoln Limited, 4 Torriano Mews
Torriano Avenue, London NW5 2RZ

www.franceslincoln.com

A catalogue record for this book is available from the British Library.

ISBN: 978-0-7112-1993-9

Set in Perpetua

Printed in Jurong Town, Singapore by Star Standard Industries in January 2010

5 7 9 8 6

a Time
Story & Pictures by
Niki Daly
F
FRANCES LINCOLN
CHILDREN'S BOOKS

When Mr Adonis said, “Children, take out your reading books,” a sick feeling would grip Sarie, making her hands tremble and her voice disappear.

Sarie hated reading aloud in class.

Those words! So many of them – running together, row after row, page after page. They tripped up her tongue. She stuttered and stammered over them. When it was her turn to read, the children in the back row giggled.

"Take your time, Sarie," Mr Adonis said kindly.

“Take your time, Sarie!” teased Charmaine and Carmen after school.
“Take your time!” joined in the smaller children.
Only Emile stood back and said nothing. He knew that Charmaine and Carmen were jealous of Sarie because she was as pretty as a princess.

At home, Sarie was called “the late lamb”, because she had been born long after her older brothers.

Her family all worked long, hard hours on the sheep farm, except on Sundays when they rested. After lunch her father took a nap, while her mother sat in the shade of the blue gum tree doing her big, loopy knitting. But after a few rows she too would fall asleep.

Then Sarie would run across the veld to the ridge. That was where Ou Missus lived. And there she would be, sitting in her rusted-up old car waiting for Sarie. Then Sarie would climb into the driver's seat and pretend to be taking a Sunday drive somewhere – far, far away.

As they drove, Ou Missus would tell stories of once upon a time, when she was young and her car was shiny. Then Sarie would tell Ou Missus everything: how she hated reading aloud, how the words stuck in her throat like dry bread, and how the children laughed at her.

"People can be cruel," said Ou Missus. "But don't give up, Sarie. It's so good to be able to read well and enjoy books."

One Sunday, tired of driving, Sarie climbed into the back. Dreamily she ran her hands over the brittle leather, into the darkness between the seat and the back-rest. Then she felt it – something under the seat. She pulled … and out came a dusty old book!

Sarie jumped into the front seat with the book. The cover creaked as she opened it.

"My goodness, Sarie!" said Ou Missus. "Look, it says '*To Lizzie with love from Mama and Papa*'. This book belonged to my daughter."

"Read it to me, read it to me!" pleaded Sarie.

The old woman shook her head. "No, Sarie!"

Sarie looked puzzled. Then Ou Missus' mouth crinkled into a smile. "We will read it together."

"Once upon a time the wife of a rich man fell ill …"

It was a lovely story about a beautiful girl and two ugly stepsisters. Reading with Ou Missus was fun. In some parts Sarie read alone. Then, just before a word could trip her up, Ou Missus would join in, until the story ended:

"*So Cinderella married her prince, and lived happily ever after.*"

As the sun dipped behind the ridge, Ou Missus closed the book. Sarie felt too happy to speak.

"It's your book now," said Ou Missus, patting Sarie's hand. "Next Sunday we will read it again."

The next day, Sarie couldn't wait to get to school. She wanted to show Mr Adonis her beautiful book.

"Ah, *Cinderella*," said Mr Adonis.

"Read it to us, sir!" cried the children.

As Mr Adonis read, Sarie remembered all of it. She could even see some of the words.

Then Mr Adonis asked the children to take out their reading books. Excitedly, Sarie opened her reading book. But when it was her turn to read aloud, the words tangled around her tongue and she started to stammer.

"Take your time, Sarie," said Mr Adonis.

Emile looked at Sarie. Her eyes filled with tears as she struggled to get the words out. Charmaine and Carmen giggled in the back row.

When Sarie saw Ou Missus, she told her all about it. "Emile is the only one who doesn't laugh," said Sarie.

"Well, he sounds like a prince," said Ou Missus. Then she clapped her hands and said, "And guess who you can be?"

She dashed into her house and came out carrying an old evening dress. It smelt musty, but it sparkled as it fell over Sarie's shoulders.

"My princess!" declared Ou Missus with a low bow.

The words poured out as clear as spring water.
"You read beautifully," said Miss November.
Out of the corner of her eye, Sarie could see Emile smiling.

After school, Sarie and Emile walked home together.

"Would you like to go for a drive in my car?" asked Sarie.

Emile laughed. "Where's your car?"

"I'll show you," said Sarie, taking his hand.

When Ou Missus saw them coming over the hill, she waved.

"Come on! Let's get going!" she shouted. Sarie jumped into the driver's seat. Ou Missus took a back seat so that Emile could sit in the front.

"So you're Emile," said Ou Missus.

"Yes," said Emile shyly. "I'm Sarie's friend."

"That's good," said Ou Missus. "Don't you think she reads beautifully?"

"Yes," said Emile.

"I bet you didn't know she could drive."

"No," giggled Emile.

“Where are we heading for, Sarie?” asked Ou Missus, settling back.

“Far, far away!” said Sarie.

Before them, the flat expanse of the Little Karoo stretched as far as the eye could see. Ridges shimmered on the hazy horizon like faraway castles. And as Sarie took the wheel, the air stood still and it seemed almost …

…Once Upon a Time.

OTHER PICTURE BOOKS IN PAPERBACK FROM FRANCES LINCOLN

JAMELA'S DRESS
Niki Daly

When Mama asks Jamela to keep an eye on her new dress material as it hangs out to dry,
Jamela can't resist wrapping it around her and dancing down the road, proud as a peacock ...
Then things go wrong, and Mama is very sad indeed, but guess who ends up with the biggest smile?
KWELA JAMELA AFRICAN QUEEN, that's who!

Suitable for National Curriculum English – Reading, Key Stage 1
Scottish Guidelines English Language – Reading, Level B; Environmental Studies, Level B

WHAT'S COOKING, JAMELA?
Niki Daly

When Mrs Zibi arrives to prepare the Christmas meal, Jamela decides to rescue Christmas, her chicken, from the pot ... and a trail of chaos follows. But, as everyone eventually agrees, "You can't eat friends!"

Suitable for National Curriculum English – Reading, Key Stages 1 and 2
Scottish Guidelines English Language, Level B/C

BRAVO ZAN ANGELO!
Niki Daly

Little Angelo longs to be a clown as famous as his grandfather, Zan Polo,
and on Carnival day in Venice he gets the chance to fulfil his wish.

Suitable for National Curriculum English – Reading, Key Stage 2
Scottish Guidelines English Language – Reading, Level C